Henny Penny

REWRITTEN BY MADGE TOVEY

ILLUSTRATED BY MARYN ROOS

Henny Penny was looking for bugs in the barnyard when a big, fat acorn fell from a tall tree and bonked her right on the head.

Henny Penny did not stop to think.

"Oh, dear!" she squawked.

"The sky is falling! The sky is falling! I must run and tell the king!"

Down the road she flew in a flurry of feathers.

As she passed the pond, she saw Ducky Lucky taking a swim.

"The sky is falling, Ducky Lucky!" she squawked. Ducky Lucky did not stop to think. "Oh, dear!" he quacked. "We must run and tell the king!"

Down the road they flew
in a flurry of feathers.

As they passed a haystack,
they saw Goosey Loosey
sitting in the shade.

"Henny Penny says that the sky is falling!" quacked Ducky Lucky.

Goosey Loosey did not stop to think. "Oh, dear!" she honked. "We must run and tell the king!"

Down the road they flew in a flurry of feathers.
As they passed a fence, they saw Cocky Locky sitting on the top rail.

"Ducky Lucky says that Henny Penny says that the sky is falling!" honked Goosey Loosey. Cocky Locky did not stop to think. "Oh, dear!" he crowed. "We must run and tell the king!"

Down the road they flew
in a flurry of feathers.

As they passed a field,
they saw Turkey Lurkey
pecking for grain.

"Goosey Loosey says that Ducky Lucky says that Henny Penny says that the sky is falling!" crowed Cocky Locky.

Turkey Lurkey did not stop to think. "Oh, dear!" he gobbled. "We must run and tell the king!"

11

Down the road they flew
in a flurry of feathers.

As they passed the
woods, Foxy Loxy came
out of his den.

"Cocky Locky says that Goosey
Loosey says that Ducky Lucky says
that Henny Penny says that the sky is
falling!" gobbled Turkey Lurkey.

Foxy Loxy did stop to think.

"We are running to tell
the king!" cackled
Henny Penny.

"Come with me,"
said Foxy Loxy.
"I know a shortcut to
the king's palace."

He opened the door to
his den. Henny Penny,
Ducky Lucky, Goosey
Loosey, Cocky Locky,
and Turkey Lurkey all
ran inside.

15

Foxy Loxy smiled as he closed the door. His long, pink tongue licked his whiskers.

Then Turkey Lurkey stopped to think.

Cocky Locky stopped to think.

Goosey Loosey stopped to think.

Ducky Lucky stopped to think.

Even Henny Penny stopped to think.

Out the door and up the road they flew in a flurry of feathers.
They did not stop until they were safe at home in the barnyard.

And Henny Penny never did tell the king that the sky was falling.

The End